*Barbie*

SISTERS
MYSTERY
CLUB
#2

THE
HAUNTED
BOARDWALK

For Elena —T.R.

Published in the United States by Random House Children's Books,
a division of Penguin Random House LLC, 1745 Broadway, New York,
NY 10019, and in Canada by Random House of Canada, a division
of Penguin Random House Ltd., Toronto. Random House and the
colophon are registered trademarks of Penguin Random House LLC.

ISBN 978-0-553-50848-2 (trade) — ISBN 978-0-375-97412-0 (lib. bdg.) —
ISBN 978-1-101-93243-8 (ebook)

randomhousekids.com

Printed in the United States of America
10 9 8 7 6 5 4 3 2 1

Random House Children's Books supports the First Amendment and
celebrates the right to read.

# Barbie

## SISTERS MYSTERY CLUB
### #2

# THE HAUNTED BOARDWALK

By Tennant Redbank

Illustrated by Artful Doodlers

Random House 🏠 New York

# PROLOGUE

One morning, on what seemed like an ordinary beach day, Barbie, Skipper, Stacie, Chelsea, and their loyal puppies were faced with a major mystery—Raquelle's missing jewelry! It was a tough case, but by working together and using their sleuthing skills, the sisters were able to track down the missing jewels—with the help of their puppies, of course.

After the case was closed, the sisters were

*determined to leave no mystery unsolved—*

*no matter how tricky. The Sisters Mystery*

*Club was formed, and no secret was safe*

*from the super sleuthing sisters!*

# CHAPTER 1

**B**arbie leaned against the wooden railing of the boardwalk. The sun was setting over the Pacific Ocean. With her sisters and their puppies, she watched the sky turn pink, orange, and crimson.

Barbie rested her chin on her hand. "Nothing is more beautiful than a California sunset," she said.

*Woof!* Taffy, Barbie's sweet pup, barked to her siblings. *"What about a brand-new bone? Bones are beautiful!"*

*"True that,"* DJ added.

Honey nodded, her ears bouncing.

Rookie just chased his own tail.

"I meant, nothing is more beautiful than our four cute little puppies!" Barbie laughed. When the puppies barked like that, it was almost as if they were talking to her! She shook her head and smiled to herself. What a silly idea—puppies couldn't talk, of course.

Barbie turned to Skipper, Stacie, and Chelsea. "So, what should we do tonight on the boardwalk?" she asked.

"Play carnival games!" Stacie said.

"The Fright Shack," Skipper suggested.

"I want to ride the Ferris wheel!" Chelsea, the youngest sister, chimed in. She shivered. "The Fright Shack is too. scary. I saw a real live ghost last time!"

"A real *live* ghost, huh?" Barbie said as she sat down on a bench.

Chelsea leaned in and whispered in Barbie's ear, "Ferris wheel!"

Barbie smiled. Getting her sisters to agree was harder than herding cats!

"Okay, we'll do *all* those things," Barbie told them. "But can we say hi to Nikki first? She's working at Crossbones tonight."

Nikki was one of Barbie's best friends. At the start of the summer, she had taken a job at a mini-golf place on the boardwalk.

Crossbones had a pirate theme. The first hole was shaped like a desert island. The fifth hole was on a pirate ship under sail. And the thirteenth hole had a treasure chest. Golfers had to send the golf ball up a ramp at the exact moment the lid of the treasure chest opened.

"Okay with me!" Stacie grinned.

Chelsea tilted her head. "Only if we go on the Ferris wheel later. Deal?"

"Deal," Barbie said.

"Hooray!" Chelsca cheered. "Come on. I know the way!" She grabbed Barbie's hand and pulled her off the bench.

"*I know the way, too!*" Honey barked to the other pups.

"*Last one to Crossbones is a poky puppy!*" DJ added.

The sisters and puppies walked by the amusement pier with its carousel, games, slide, and, of course, the Ferris wheel.

Next to the amusement pier was Crossbones. Barbie, her sisters, and the puppies stopped outside. Usually Crossbones was full of people lining up to play, picking out colored golf balls, and putting on the green Astroturf. But tonight it was empty.

Over the entrance, a single light flickered. Two other bulbs were dark.

Chelsea grabbed Skipper's hand. "This is even spookier than the Fright Shack!" she said with a shiver.

Barbie frowned. Chelsea was right. It *was* spooky. Something seemed wrong.

Rookie let out a long, low howl.

*"Shhh,"* Taffy hushed him. *"Don't scare them!"*

"Nikki?" Barbie called. There was no answer. Barbie called again.

She heard a clatter behind the wooden counter. Dark-brown hair popped up above the register. It was Nikki!

"Barbie? Is that you?" Nikki said. "I'm so glad you're here! Something weird is going on. I think Crossbones is haunted!"

# CHAPTER 2

"**H**aunted?" Barbie blinked.

Nikki nodded. "I know it sounds crazy," she said. "But you wouldn't *believe* what I've seen tonight!"

She came out from behind the counter. "It all started right after Marcus left. Marcus is the guy who works the shift before mine," she explained. "Lots of people were here golfing. But then things started to go wrong."

"What do you mean 'wrong'?" Skipper asked.

"The holes. You know a lot of them have moving parts, right?" Nikki said.

Stacie nodded. "Like the pirate ship!"

"And the treasure chest!" Chelsea added. "That's my favorite."

"Anyway, the pirate ship . . ." Nikki paused. "Maybe I should just show you." She led Barbie and her sisters onto the mini-golf course. The puppies followed them. Nikki cut across a couple of holes to hole five. "See? Look at that!"

An eight-foot-tall pirate ship stood at the center of the hole. Usually it swayed back and forth over wooden waves. But tonight it jerked violently from side to side, creaking loudly.

DJ backed away from it and growled.

Taffy barked. *"Keep still, you crazy ship!"*

The ship did look spooky. Still, that didn't mean it was haunted. "Maybe it's just broken," Barbie said.

"That's what I thought, too," Nikki said. "But come see hole eight!"

They moved down the course. As they got closer, Barbie felt water mist her face.

"Hey!" Chelsea said. "Is it raining?"

"It's not rain," Nikki told them. She gestured to hole eight. From the back of a plaster whale spurted a waterspout. Normally the waterspout was a light spray of water rising five feet. Now it soared fifteen feet into the air!

"It's not just these two holes either," Nikki said. "It's all over the course. The golfers got freaked out. They left!"

"A spouting whale isn't a ghost,"

Barbie said to Nikki.

"But look at that!" Nikki pointed to hole number nine. Standing in front of a cave was an eerie green skeleton.

Stacie gulped. "Uh, Nikki, isn't that skeleton usually white?" she asked.

"Yes," said Nikki.

*"I like all sorts of bones,"* Rookie barked to the pups. *"But not green ones!"*

Honey hid her nose under her paws.

"If it were just one hole," Nikki said, "I'd understand. But it's the *entire* course!"

Chelsea gasped and covered her mouth.

The skeleton was moving!

"Beware!" the skeleton warned them in a mechanical voice. "Beware! Beware! BEWARE!" Then the skeleton started to laugh.

"Ahhhh!" Chelsea screamed. She turned and ran away!

# CHAPTER 3

"Chelsea! Wait!" Barbie shouted.

Stacie and Rookie dashed after Chelsea. Stacie was the fastest kid on her soccer team and easily caught up to her little sister.

"It's okay!" she told Chelsea. "Remember, the skeleton *always* says 'Beware!'"

Chelsea shook her head. She paused. Then she nodded. "That's right! He does always say that. I forgot!"

Barbie, Skipper, and Nikki ran up to them. Honey put her paws on Chelsea's knees. *"You okay?"* she barked.

"I wasn't afraid," Chelsea said. "I just . . . *felt* like running."

Another noise caught Barbie's ear. What was it? She raised a finger to her lips. "Shhh," she said. "I hear something."

They all fell quiet. Barbie heard a *creak.* She heard a *hiss.* She heard a long scratching sound.

Honey stopped sniffing. Taffy's ears perked up.

For a few seconds, no one said anything. Then Stacie asked, "Wh-what is that?" Her voice trembled.

Nikki looked over her shoulder. "I forgot to tell you. It's not just weird things happening at the golf holes. It's also these strange noises. I've been hearing them all night! Hissing. Bumps. And scratchy-scratchy sounds, like claws dragged across stone. It's really creeping me out!"

"Between this place and the Fright Shack," Stacie said, "I think the whole boardwalk is haunted!"

"I don't know what's going on, Nikki," Barbie said. "But the Sisters Mystery Club will help you find out!"

Nikki flashed them a smile. "Just don't leave me alone with the ghost!"

Chelsea tugged on Skipper's hand. "I think I just heard the pirate on hole twelve *meow*!" she whispered.

Skipper raised an eyebrow. Barbie, Stacie, and Nikki looked at each other. They burst out laughing.

"Don't worry, Nikki," Barbie said. "We'll figure out what's haunting Crossbones!"

"And the rest of the boardwalk!" Chelsea added.

"Let's make a plan," Skipper said. She looked at some flat rocks next to hole thirteen. "We can sit there."

"Perfect!" Nikki said. She walked over and cleaned some litter off the rocks— a plastic bottle, napkins, and an empty bag of pet treats. Tossing them in a trash can, she waved to her friends to sit down. The puppies curled up by their feet.

Skipper took out her smartphone. She pulled up a page on ghosts. "Ghosts are usually found at really old places," she said. "How old is Crossbones?"

Nikki frowned. "It was built five years ago, I think."

Skipper shook her head. She looked back at her phone. "Um, have there been any accidents here?" she asked.

"*No!*" Nikki said. "At least, I don't think so. Someone slipped on the sidewalk and twisted an ankle. And once I found a dead mouse by the back gate. But that doesn't count, right? A mouse couldn't haunt a mini-golf place."

"Oooh!" Chelsea giggled. "A ghost mouse! Awesome."

"Just picture its itty-bitty ghost whiskers and ghost tail," Stacie curled her hands and wiggled her nose. "I've come for your cheeeeeeese!"

Barbie laughed. She had two very silly sisters! "Does it say anything about how to catch a ghost?" she asked Skipper.

Skipper scrolled down the page. "Hmm," she said. "You can use an EMF detector. That picks up on changes in the electrical magnetic field. Or you can look for cold spots—"

"It *was* awfully cold by hole two," Nikki broke in.

"Or . . ." Skipper jumped to her feet. "Yes! This is it! This is how we'll catch the ghost. We'll set a trap!"

# CHAPTER 4

"**A** trap?" Barbie asked. "What kind of trap?"

"A video trap," Skipper said. "We'll leave my phone by one of the holes. I'll put it on record. It will show us anything that goes by; whether it's a real person messing with you, Nikki—"

"Or a ghost!" Stacie finished for her.

Skipper flicked her phone to video mode. She put it on the flat rock by hole thirteen and pointed it toward the treasure chest. Then she tapped the phone to record.

"I doubt the ghost will come if we're here," Barbie said.

"You're right," Nikki said. "We can wait at the golf hut." She led them to a tiki-style hut near the entrance. When she opened the door, the puppies rushed inside. Barbie and her sisters followed them.

Barbie looked around. The golf hut was cozy, but her fingers itched to decorate it. With some cute curtains and a fluffy rug, it would be the perfect spot to hang out!

"Are you hungry? Thirsty?" Nikki asked.

"We have snacks." She waved at a shelf on the wall. On it were bottles of water, bags of chips, a couple of oranges, and three rows of cans stacked five high.

"What's with all the tuna fish?" Skipper asked.

Nikki laughed. "Crazy, right?" Nikki said. "Marcus brings it. It's his favorite snack, I guess."

Skipper and Chelsea split an orange and a bottle of water. Barbie and Nikki chatted about a charity event they were throwing the following week. Stacie grabbed three golf balls off the counter.

"Watch this," she told Nikki. "I learned to juggle a few weeks ago." She tossed the balls into the air. For about thirty seconds, she did great. Then she missed one, and it dropped to the ground. Rookie chased it across the floor.

"Butterfingers!" Skipper said.

Stacie shrugged. "It's not easy. Try it!" She held out the golf balls.

"I'll stick to computer programming, thank you!" Skipper said.

"And catching ghosts on a haunted boardwalk!" Chelsea said.

"Speaking of that . . ." Barbie glanced at the clock on the wall. "It's been about forty minutes. Should we check the phone?"

"Yeah!" Stacie said.

The puppies perked up. They had lost interest in chewing on an old shoe. *"We're going out!"* Taffy barked to her siblings.

*"Walkies!"* Honey added.

Barbie led the way back to hole thirteen.

"Uh-oh," Skipper said when they got close. Her phone wasn't how she had left it. It was facedown on the rock.

She turned it over. "Phew! It's not broken!" She hit play. The screen showed the treasure chest opening and closing. Skipper fast-forwarded.

"Wait!" Barbie leaned in closer. "Go back. I think I saw something."

Skipper moved the video back a few

minutes and played it again. At the seventeen-minute mark, a shadow crossed the screen.

"The ghost!" Chelsea cried.

Barbie frowned. "I don't know. It's so dark. I can't—"

From the phone came a howl. Dark shapes darted past the screen, too close to make out. The image shook wildly. Then the video went black.

"That must be when the phone fell over," Skipper said.

"You mean when the ghost *pushed* it

over!" Chelsea said.

"See?" Nikki said. "That proves it. Crossbones really *is* haunted!"

*"I knew it!"* DJ barked to the other pups.

Barbie stared at Skipper's cell phone. Sure, something strange was going on. The weird noises. The green skeleton. The waterspout and the rocking ship. But haunted? She wasn't convinced. "I wish there were some other way to watch the course," she said.

"How? The ghost won't come while we're here," Stacie said.

Barbie barely heard Stacie. Her mind was running through ideas. "If only we could see the whole thing," she said. "If only—" She lifted her eyes above the pirate ship, above the waterspout, above the mini-golf course, to the sky.

Everything clicked into place. "That's it!" She turned to Chelsea. "Guess what?" she said. "We're going on the Ferris wheel!"

# CHAPTER 5

Chelsea did a little dance. Honey spun in a circle, too.

"Woo-hoo!" Chelsea cried. "We're riding the Ferris wheel! We're riding the Ferris wheel!" Then she stopped. She looked thoughtful. "Wait. What about the ghost?"

Skipper nodded. "I get it," she said. "The Ferris wheel is right next to Crossbones. We'll get a perfect view from up there!"

"Exactly," Barbie said.

"Great idea!" Nikki said. "Just let me lock up."

While Nikki pulled the gate closed, Skipper led the way to the amusement pier.

"Five tickets for the Ferris wheel," Barbie told the man at the ticket booth. "Can we take our puppies on board?"

The man leaned over the counter and looked down at the puppies.

"*Look cute,*" Taffy told the other pups.

"*And small,*" Honey added.

"*And well-behaved,*" Rookie put in.

*"Set your puppy-dog eyes to stun!"* DJ looked up at the ticket-seller and blinked. Puppy-dog eyes were irresistible to humans.

"Aw, sure. Why not?" the ticket-seller said. "Do you want tickets for the Fright Shack, too?"

"No, thanks," Chelsea told him. "We're taking on one haunted place at a time!"

The man handed them five tickets just as Nikki got there.

"Ready to catch a ghost?" Barbie asked.

"Ready!" Skipper, Stacie, Chelsea, and Nikki said together.

The line for the Ferris wheel was short. After a ten-minute wait, they reached the front. A purple car stopped for them.

"Yay! Purple!" Chelsea said. She scrambled inside. Barbie climbed into the car after her, carrying Taffy. Nikki, Skipper, and Stacie sat across from them. Each had a puppy on her lap.

Chelsea wiggled impatiently. "Why does it keep stopping?" she asked.

"They load the cars one by one," Skipper said.

"When everyone is on board, it will go faster," Barbie told her. "See?" Barbie added as the Ferris wheel picked up speed. Their car lifted higher into the air.

"I see Crossbones!" Stacie said. The car passed the top. Then it started going down the other side.

Barbie's heart beat faster. She didn't believe in ghosts, but she still couldn't wait to discover what was haunting the mini-golf course.

"Something is moving down there!" Skipper said.

"I see it, too!" Nikki said. "But it's really dark."

Their car dropped lower. The mini-golf course disappeared behind trees.

"Argh," Skipper said. "I couldn't tell what it was."

"Next time around," Nikki said. The car revolved past the bottom and began to rise again.

"Okay," Barbie said. "Everyone, look closely!" Crossbones came into view.

"Yes! I see it!" Stacie said.

"Lots of things are moving on the course," Skipper said. "I don't think they're ghosts."

"They're too little," Chelsea added.

Once again, the car dropped past where they could see Crossbones.

The Ferris wheel turned. Their car

passed the boarding platform. It rose into the air.

"We're almost at the top," Barbie said. "Can you see anything?"

"Shapes! Shadows!" Stacie said. "What *are* they?"

"We're going to miss it!" Nikki said.

Suddenly, the car stopped. It rocked back and forth.

*"Whee!"* Rookie barked. *"This is fun!"*

"They must be unloading people," Barbie said. "This is our chance!"

She narrowed her eyes. Dark shapes

crisscrossed the mini-golf course. Chelsea was right. They were too small to be people. Or ghosts. Unless they were ghosts of giant mice as Stacie had joked earlier. Or . . .

"Cats!" Barbie cried. "I think they're cats!"

# CHAPTER 6

The Ferris wheel began moving again. This time, when their car reached the bottom, it stopped. Nikki, Barbie, her sisters, and the puppies got off.

"Cats?" Nikki said as they left the amusement pier. "I'm not sure I understand."

Chelsea crossed her arms. "I told you I heard a *meow*," she said. "You just *laughed* at me!"

"Oh, Chelsea, I'm sorry," Barbie said.

"You were right!"

Rookie romped over to Crossbones. *"Let me in! I have ghosts . . . uh, I mean, cats to catch!"*

Nikki unlocked the gate to the mini-golf course. They went inside.

"I've been thinking about it, and I have an idea," Skipper said. "Where are the electronic parts of the golf holes?"

"We control them by computer," Nikki said. "But some of the switches and wires run behind the holes. I'll show you."

Then, Chelsea shrieked. "Something brushed my leg!"

Skipper turned on her cell phone flashlight. It shone off a pair of green eyes. "A cat!" she said.

The cat blinked at them and ran off.

*"Did you see that?"* Taffy barked to the other pups.

*"I can't believe we thought a few cats were a ghost."* DJ hung his head.

*"My sniffer must be broken,"* Honey wailed.

Skipper knelt down by the switches.

"Aha!" she said. "Lots of these are out of place! The cats must have been stepping on them. Like the switch for hole nine. It's set to a green light, not white. That's why the skeleton was green!"

"And that's not all," Barbie said. She pointed to the ground next to the switches. Several empty cans of tuna fish were scattered around.

"I don't get it," Stacie said. "Tuna fish? But why would—"

Nikki laughed. "Tuna fish!" she said. "Marcus! You know, the guy who works here? He loves animals. He has three dogs and two birds at home. I bet he was feeding the stray cats! That's why he had so much tuna fish in the hut."

"He totally picked the wrong spot to feed them," Skipper said. "Of course some of the cats would step on the switches!"

"Marcus's heart was in the right place," Barbie said. "But I know a better way to take care of them. We can take them—"

"To the animal shelter!" Stacie finished for her.

Nikki nodded. "Great idea! The vet

there will give them the shots they need. And find them good homes."

"Homes with lots and lots of tuna fish," Chelsea said.

"I'll get Marcus to help me round up the cats tomorrow," Nikki said.

"Can we help?" Stacie asked.

"Of course!" Nikki said.

Chelsea frowned. "Does this mean the

Fright Shack isn't haunted either?" she asked.

Skipper shrugged. "Who knows?"

"Maybe that's the next mystery for the Sisters Mystery Club to solve!" Stacie said.

The puppies barked. *More mysteries? That sounded fun!*

Barbie put her arms around Skipper's and Stacie's shoulders. "Well, what do you want to do now?"

"Games!" Stacie said.

"Ice cream," Skipper said.

"The Ferris wheel!" Chelsea said.

Barbie looked at Chelsea. "AGAIN?" she asked.

"Again!" Chelsea said.